For Connor and Brendan, and for Billy, the brightest stars in my sky —M.L.

For my friends and family who brighten my holidays —N.M.

Clarion Books is an imprint of HarperCollins Publishers.

Twinkle, Twinkle, Winter Night
Text copyright © 2022 by Megan Litwin
Illustrations copyright © 2022 by Nneka Myers

ISBN 978-0-35-857204-6

The artist used Procreate, Photoshop, and holiday cheer to create the illustrations for this book.
Typography by Celeste Knudsen
22 23 24 25 26 RTLO 10 9 8 7 6 5 4 3 2 1

First Edition

Twinkle, Twinkle, Winter Night

by Megan Litwin * Illustrated by Nneka Myers

Clarion Books
An Imprint of HarperCollins Publishers

Twinkle, twinkle, winter night.
Everywhere you look there's light.

Come along to see the show.
Nightfall sets the world aglow.

Rising slowly overhead,
moon tucks daylight into bed.

In the quiet, calm, and clear—

sky sparkles like a chandelier.

Shimmer,
glimmer,
glowing
light—

twinkle, twinkle,
winter night.

Snowflakes join the soundless show,
hushing up the world below.

Dusting glitter on earth's face,
dressing trees in coats of lace.

Peaceful,
perfect,
silent,
white—

twinkle, twinkle,
winter night.

More magic lies just further on,
only seen from dusk 'til dawn.

From quiet wood
to busy town,

look up,
look down,
look all around.

Houses wear their very best,
each one different from the rest.

Some have brilliant colored lights,
others creamy, dreamy whites.

Beaming,
gleaming,
lively sight—

twinkle,
twinkle,
winter night.

Pathways beckon
bright and bold,
windows wink with
eyes of gold.

A candle here, eight more there,
for all to see,
and all to share.

Darkness,
dazzle,
warmth,
delight—

twinkle, twinkle, winter night.

Now off to cozy beds to sleep,
bundled, burrowed, snug and deep.

The feathered, furry, tall, and small—
sweet dreams of light to one and all.

Magic,
wonder,
beauty
bright—

twinkle right on
through the night.

Twinkle, twinkle, winter night.
Everywhere you look . . .

there's LIGHT.